Best Friends

Elisabeth Reuter

First published in German under the title: Judith and Lisa
© Copyright 1988 Verlag Heinrich Ellermann, Munchen

© Copyright 1993 **Yellow Brick Road Press**
Printed in Germany

ISBN: 0-943706-18-1

Dear Children,

This is a story about friendship and much more. It is based on the experiences of many children. It is a story that you should read with your parents, and your friends.

In 1938, an evil dictator, Adolf Hitler, began persuading the German people that all their problems were due to the Jews. Many people in Germany were poor at that time, and many were angry because they didn't have jobs. They wanted very much to blame someone for their difficult lives. Hitler knew this and convinced the German people that they were "special", better than anyone else, especially the Jews. He told them that it was the Jews who were keeping them from becoming a great and powerful people, and that if they destroyed the Jews all their troubles would go away.

Many German children learned from their parents and teachers that they too were "special". They were taught that the Jews were trying to ruin their minds, and souls, by writing bad books and painting bad pictures. They were taught that it was because of the Jews that life was so difficult in Germany.

Some children, like the German girl in the story, didn't want to feel more important if it meant mistreating their Jewish classmates. But hearing the same lies over and over again affected even the nicest German children, until they too began to believe that all the Jews were their enemies.

In this story we see what happens when people allow themselves to believe lies and to be led astray. We see what happens when people do not stand firm against what they know to be evil and falsehood.

Best Friends will make you feel. It will make you think. It is a story of what happened not so long ago. And it is a warning of what can happen if we allow ourselves to feel more important than others.

The Translators

Judith and Lisa lived in Germany. They were the best friends anyone could ever imagine. They lived across the street from each other. They laughed and played together. Sometimes they were sad together. From time to time they also quarrelled with each other. But they always became friends again quickly because they loved each other very much.

Lisa and Judith sat next to each other in school. One day, a large picture was hung on the wall above the teacher's desk. Another picture was hung on each side of the classroom. The pictures showed a man with a little mustache. Judith's father had said that this man was something like a wicked emperor. Because of him, children and adults no longer said "Good morning" to each other. Instead, they said, "Heil Hitler!".

At school, the children learned to read and write. They learned arithmetic, music and many other subjects. Now Judith and Lisa were also taught that good people had blonde hair and blue eyes. Good people were strong and German. There were bad people, too, the teacher told them. The bad people had hooked noses, dark hair and a cunning look in their eyes. They were the Jews.

"The Jews are a great threat to the German people," warned the teacher. "We would be much better off if there weren't any Jews at all" she told them.

Judith kept quiet. Just the other day, her father had said to her mother, "They won't do us any harm, even though we are Jews." "They" were the men wearing black boots and brown shirts and the man with the small mustache.

Judith was confused. She touched her dark, braided hair and looked self-consciously at the teacher.

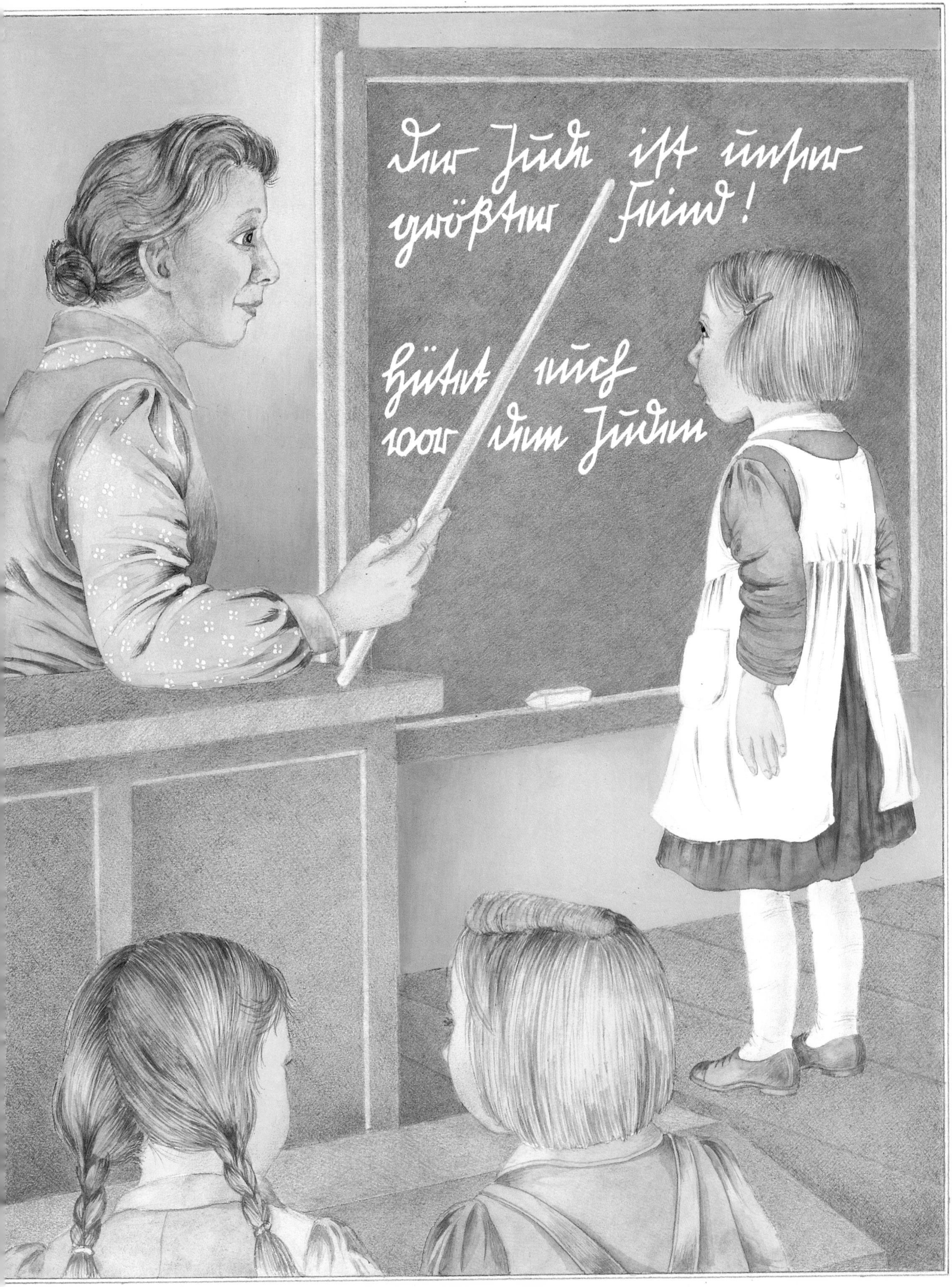
Der Jude ist unser größter Feind!
Hütet euch vor dem Juden

The men with the black boots and brown shirts marched through the streets very often. They wanted everyone to believe that the man with the small mustache -- the one they called Hitler -- was the greatest leader in the world. When they marched, people lined the streets waving flags and shouting, "Heil Hitler!"

Judith would have liked to wave a small flag too, but her parents had forbidden her to have a flag with a swastika on it, the symbol of Hitler and his followers. But one day, a friendly old man bent down and gave Judith a flag.

The children learned there were bad books, most of which had been written by Jews. To prevent the children's souls from being poisoned, all these books had to be burned. The teacher also told them that there would be no more bad pictures or bad music because the artists and musicians, who were all Jewish, were no longer allowed to paint or play their instruments. Judith and Lisa, like all the children in the class, were told to look at the pictures hanging on the walls in their home and tell the teacher whether their parents had any bad pictures painted by Jews.

Soon, almost all of the children in the class began to feel very proud and sure of themselves. It felt good to have someone to blame for everything that went wrong. Perhaps it was the Jews' fault that children had so little to eat at snack time, that they got so few presents on their birthdays, that their fathers could not find jobs and that they lived in such small apartments. Maybe it would be much better if there were no Jews.

Judith was no longer happy at school.

Lisa was now the only one who would speak to Judith and their lives were getting more and more difficult.

"Move to the back of the class, Judith," the teacher said, and Judith had to sit in the back of the classroom all alone. The other children stared at her.

During recess the children surrounded Judith and shouted, "Jewish girl! Jewish girl!". Lisa ran to Judith and put her arm around her to protect her. This made the children stop yelling at her.

Judith was no longer allowed to go swimming with Lisa, nor to gymnastics. Many restaurants put up signs saying, "No Jews Allowed", and one day a sign appeared on the pharmacy that belonged to Judith's parents. It said, "Germans, protect yourselves. Do not buy from Jews."

Lisa was very confused because she liked Judith so much and Judith's parents were always so kind and friendly to her. She could not understand why everyone was treating Judith so badly just because she was Jewish.

"How does being Jewish make Judith different from me?" Lisa asked her mother.

Instead of an answer, her mother pleaded with her to stop playing with Judith. "There are many other children, good German children, you can play with," she told her, anxiously.

Now Lisa's mother no longer went to Judith's parents' pharmacy. Instead, she bought what she needed at another pharmacy several blocks away.

Judith and Lisa had to invent secret hand signals if they wanted to visit each other. They would signal to each other from the window or the balcony. Waving three times meant, "I'm coming to play" and showing a fist three times meant, "You'd better not come now, my parents are home."

"Don't speak with Judith anymore," begged Lisa's mother, "You are inviting trouble." Lisa did not understand why her mother was afraid.

"Don't ask so many questions," her father warned her, "You are too young to understand. We just have to be careful these days."

One afternoon Lisa gave Judith the all-clear signal that they could play together. What they liked doing best was acting out stories about the three bears in the woods. They each had a bear. Pooh belonged to Judith and Jojo belonged to Lisa. Woody was the smallest bear and they both liked to play with him the best.

It was a strange sort of day and Lisa suddenly felt different from Judith. "From now on, only I am allowed to play with Woody," she declared. When Judith objected, Lisa suddenly blurted out, "You are just a Jewish girl anyway!"

A sad silence settled over them.

Judith dropped Woody and stood up. Picking up her bear, Pooh, she ran as fast as she could down the stairs. Lisa stayed behind all alone. Angry and embarrassed, she shouted insults at Judith and flung the bears with all her might into the corner.

Judith did not come to school the next day. Nor the day after. The following day she was absent too. Nobody mentioned her anymore. It was as though she had never lived.

Lisa was sorry about their fight over Woody, but Judith didn't come to the window anymore. No matter how much she pleaded, Lisa's parents absolutely forbade her to go to Judith's house.

One night while Lisa was fast asleep with Woody in her arms, the Nazis, the men in the black boots and brown shirts, came to destroy everything owned by Jews. Stores, synagogues and schools were wrecked.

Lisa did not hear the noise of the car engines as they screeched to a halt in front of the buildings. She did not hear the heavy sound of boots as the Nazis ran to do their work. Nor did she hear the shouting and the screaming as Jewish store owners protested and were dragged away with their families.

Lisa slept peacefully. Nothing woke her, not even the crashing and shattering of glass as the Nazis smashed and destroyed everything they could get their hands on.

This night came to be known as Kristallnacht (Night of Broken Glass) because of the sound of shattering glass as windows were broken in all the synagogues and Jewish stores throughout Germany.

In the morning, when Lisa went to the window and looked across the street at Judith's house, she gasped with horror. She saw that the pharmacy had been completely destroyed. The windows were smashed. There was broken glass everywhere. Inside the store the cabinets and display cases had been knocked over and bottles, boxes, paper, and medicine were scattered all over the floor. The front door was hanging wide open and on the sidewalk were broken pill bottles, file papers and furniture, all trampled and broken.

Lisa was frightened. She felt her heart pounding. She ran out onto the street, still holding Woody. She stopped in the middle of all the broken glass and screamed for Judith. But Judith didn't answer.

"Lisa, wait!" called her mother, running after her. "Come back here, they've all gone!"

"Gone?" asked Lisa, terrified, as she peered into the dark entrance of the store. "Where have they gone? I want to give Woody back to Judith. I want to make friends with her again."

"They are not coming back," whispered her mother, tugging impatiently at Lisa's arm. But Lisa did not move. She just stood there, staring. "There's Pooh," she pointed to Judith's teddy bear. He was lying in the middle of pieces of broken glass. The soldiers had walked all over him with their muddy boots.

Something terrible had happened but Lisa could not understand what it was. She dropped Woody next to Judith's bear and looked at her mother. "Don't think about it, just forget everything," said Lisa's mother. She grasped Lisa's arm and forced her back into the house.

Shortly afterwards, the children learned at school that it would be better if the Jews wore a special sign on their clothing so that people would know they were Jews. This was important because some Jews pretended to be just like other people. And, in fact, one day all the Jews did have to wear a sign – a big yellow star – on their clothing whenever they went outside.

Lisa thought that now she would find Judith. She looked very carefully at every little girl wearing a yellow star. She looked wherever she went. But though she searched very hard, she never, ever found Judith again.